ALEX FITZGERALD'S
Cure for Nightmares

by Kathleen Krull
illustrated by Wendy Edelson

Troll

To Jacqui and Melanie
K.K.

Something grabs my hand. I try to run, but I'm frozen. Slowly I turn around . . . and see them. Monsters. Six eyes, hairy noses, and black lips. Monsters . . . from outer space . . . yanking me toward them . . .

Alexandra Fitzgerald woke up in a cold sweat. "Yikes, another nightmare," she groaned.

Her third one this week!

Wait just a minute. Those monsters looked really familiar.

Alex sat up in bed. Where had she seen these creatures before?

Oh, right—they were the *Aliens You Love to Hate.*

Alex hadn't seen the movie. She hated scary movies. But she *had* seen the lunch box. Her new California best friend, Becky Garcia, had one.

"You baby!" Alex whispered. "A nightmare about lunch boxes!" No way could she tell anybody about this. Even Becky would laugh at her.

Alex looked around for familiar things: her stuffed animals, her five Barbie dolls, her stack of piano music.

This wasn't really a bedroom. It was her dad's office. He wrote books about weird and wonderful ways to lose weight. In the corner was a futon that Alex used as a bed.

Alex's parents were divorced. Normally, she lived with her mother in Chicago. Normally, her mother had a great job there. But then she got transferred to Japan for a year. So Alex was living with her father this year.

And California was not normal. Palm trees, for instance, were *so* weird looking. Naturally, her dad lived in an apartment complex called Palm Tree Heaven.

And now these nightmares. What normal nine-year-old kid has bad dreams practically every night?

Alex wasn't feeling scared anymore. On her way to the bathroom, she almost bumped into her dad.

"Good morning!" he said. "How about a mushroom milk shake for breakfast?"

"Yikes—no, thanks, Dad," said Alex. "Just some doughnuts, please."

"You look a little pale," her dad said. "You sleep okay?"

"Just fine," Alex lied. She didn't know how to explain about the nightmares. Maybe she'd get scared all over again if she talked about them. Maybe her dad would laugh at her. Maybe he'd suggest mushroom milk shakes as a cure.

"Mushrooms for breakfast make me feel a little sick," Alex said.

"Sorry," her dad said. "I wish you felt the same way about doughnuts. All those calories!"

Still, he had a box of delicious doughnuts. Alex ate three—peanut butter, powdered sugar, and chocolate. Then she gathered her school things and ran out the door to meet Becky by the gate.

"See you later, Dad," called Alex. "Don't forget—tryouts this afternoon for the Christmas play. I'll be home later than usual."

"Good luck!" he called back.

Alex and Becky walked the three blocks to Ocean View School. Alex tried not to look at too many palm trees. She saw bright flowers that looked like they were

from outer space. She saw real oranges and lemons hanging from the trees.

But it was late September. Something was missing.

"When do the trees change color?" she asked Becky.

"This is it, Fitzgerald," said Becky. "It's the same here all year round. You'll get used to it."

"How can I get used to no snow at Christmas?" asked Alex.

"No problem. Colin Ward is in charge of fake snow for our Christmas play," Becky said. "His mom gets it from the movie studio where she works. I'll check the list—it's in here."

She set her lunch box down on the sidewalk and opened it up.

Alex began to giggle. "Fake snow!"

Then she was looking at the *Aliens You Love to Hate* on Becky's lunch box. She wasn't scared a bit right now. But last night . . .

Alex just hoped Becky and the other kids wouldn't find out. California was weird enough. Being known as a *baby* here would make it much worse. She'd have to find a cure for nightmares, that's all.

"Hey, Fitzgerald—*why* are you staring at my lunch box?" asked Becky.

Alex felt herself turning beet red. She had to think fast. "Well, your lunch box reminds me of weird California!" she said.

"You'll get used to it," Becky said again. She put her list back in her lunch box. "Right. Fake snow for the Christmas play. You'll have a white Christmas for sure, Fitzgerald."

The two girls started off on the last block to school.

Alex liked Ocean View School. It really did have an ocean view. But that day Alex and Becky didn't notice the bright blue sky and pounding surf. They were too excited. They couldn't stop thinking about the try-outs for the fourth-grade Christmas play.

Ms. Chung, the music teacher, was directing the play. She'd written beautiful music for it.

Becky took ballet lessons every Saturday morning. She was eager to be a dancer in the show.

Alex was almost positive she'd be chosen to play piano. After all, back in Chicago she was Mrs. Pinkowski's star pupil.

Finally, the last class of the day was over. Alex and Becky punched each other lightly on the arm for good luck. Then they went to separate rooms for their tryouts.

Alex didn't know her way around her new school too well yet. But she found Room 202 at last. She went in and sat down.

There were four kids trying out to play

piano for the show. Three boys and Alex.

Alex had seen one of the boys around school. His name was Elan Kent. Every day he wore a T-shirt that said something different. Today he wore a pink shirt that said NOT WHEN THE SURF'S UP.

Alex thought he probably spent more time surfing than playing the piano. He made a lot of mistakes.

So did the other two boys. It was her turn. She'd been practicing hard. She didn't make a single mistake.

"Excellent!" said Ms. Chung.

Alex glowed. Elan Kent looked mad.

"Thank you all very much," Ms. Chung said. "Next Monday morning I will announce the entire cast and stage crew for the play. You will find out then whom I've picked to play piano for the show."

Alex went to find Becky. On the way home, the two girls sang Christmas songs from the play.

Alex couldn't wait until Monday. She just knew she had passed the tryout. She knew it.

But one morning she woke up and wasn't so sure.

I'm in Room 202 again. This time, instead of playing the piano, we each have to shinny up a palm tree! One boy after another goes up and down the tree. Ms. Chung shouts, "Excellent!" Then it's my turn.

But palm trees have no branches to hold on to. Each time I get a grip on the tree, I slide right back down again. I hate palm trees. Ms. Chung frowns. Elan Kent points his finger at me. He wears his yellow T-shirt that says SURF CITY. *He whispers, "Baby!" Then everyone is saying it: "Baby, baby, baby!"*

Alex felt sick. *Another* nightmare!

As usual, she passed her dad on the way to the bathroom.

"Good morning," he said. "Alex, what's the matter? You look terrible. Come into the kitchen. I'll fix you some mushroom muffins."

Alex said no thanks to the muffins. But she went into the kitchen and sat down.

She took a deep breath. "I've been having bad dreams lately," she said.

"What kind of bad dreams?" her dad asked.

"Silly things," said Alex. "Like monsters. Monsters from a *lunch box*. Palm trees. Tryouts to climb palm trees."

"That doesn't sound silly," he said. "In a dream, almost anything can be scary. But it's only a dream, Alex. It's not really real, you know."

Alex fetched a raspberry doughnut from the cupboard. "I know," she said. "But I still get scared. Then I feel like a baby. Only babies have so many nightmares."

"Grown-ups have nightmares, too," her dad said. "Dreams are just tricks. They're tricks our minds play while we are sleeping. Anyone can have good or bad ones."

Alex thought about that. "But how can I stop having the bad ones all the time? Can you help me find a cure?"

"I can try," he said. "Let's leave the light

on in your room. If you have a bad dream, you can wake up and see where you are. It will make you feel safe."

"Sounds good!" said Alex.

So she tried it that night. She said good night to her Barbie dolls, her stuffed animals, and her dad. With the light still on, she curled up on the futon. She shut her eyes.

After a while, she opened her eyes. Five pairs of eyes stared back at her—her Barbie dolls!

Alex looked away. The beady eyes of her stuffed animals watched her.

On the closet doors were two doorknobs. They looked like two more big eyes.

She rolled over. Now she was facing her dad's computer. Its knobs and dials stared at her.

Alex tried thinking of it as a friendly robot saying, "Go to sleep, Alex!"

So Alex did. But before she did, she

reached over and turned the light off. Now nothing could stare at her. This idea hadn't worked at all!

Alex got up early for school the next morning. She forgot all about everything staring at her.

It was Monday morning. Time to find out who made the tryouts!

Alex and Becky raced the three blocks to school. Outside Room 202, Ms. Chung was reading off names.

". . . Caitlin Williams, Colin Ward, Emily Appelbaum, and Rebecca Garcia," Ms. Chung said. "Those will be the dancers for the play."

Becky grabbed Alex. Alex hugged her back.

Ms. Chung read the names of other performers and the stage crew. The kids on the stage crew would get costumes ready and move scenery around. Elan Kent was

on the stage crew. Today he wore a T-shirt that said HEAVEN IS ONLY AN OCEAN AWAY.

Then Ms. Chung said, "We will have a piano solo in the play. It will feature Alexandra Fitzgerald."

Alex grabbed Becky. The two girls whirled around. Alex saw Elan whisper something to the boy next to him.

"Quiet, please," Ms. Chung said. "Our first rehearsal will be after school next Monday. I expect everyone to be on time."

Alex was so happy she could hardly pay attention. She felt like a real part of her new school. She felt very grown-up.

Then she remembered her nightmares. Her dad's cure hadn't really done anything to help. But maybe they were over once and for all.

Alex hoped so. She didn't want babyish bad dreams to spoil her new life.

Alex stayed at Becky's house on Halloween.

It was Alex's first slumber party. Besides Becky and Alex, there were Caitlin Williams and Emily Appelbaum. Everyone except Alex dressed up as a dancer to go trick-or-treating. Alex went as a snowman.

The girls brought their bags of treats back to Becky's house.

"Let's watch a movie," Caitlin said.

"No problem!" said Becky. "My mom rented *Dracula* for us."

"I hate scary movies," said Alex. "Maybe I'll just go upstairs to bed."

Both Caitlin and Emily screamed with laughter.

"You can't go to *bed* at a slumber party," Caitlin said. "Don't you have slumber parties back in Chicago?"

"Of course we do," said Alex. "I was just kidding around."

"Don't worry, Fitzgerald," said Becky. "It's just an old monster movie. And my parents are right in the kitchen."

"So Dracula won't get you," Emily said. She raised her arms and lunged toward Alex.

"Yikes!" said Alex. She giggled weakly.

But she didn't enjoy the movie. The other girls squealed and pretended to be scared. Alex didn't see what was so funny about vampires. Even old ones with phony makeup.

Alex was glad when Becky's parents

came in with a pizza. She loved pizza. Then the movie was finally over. The four girls went upstairs to Becky's room. They put on pajamas. They got into their sleeping bags. It was almost eleven o'clock.

They talked about school and the Christmas play.

"Alex, your piano piece is the greatest," said Emily. "Don't you think so, Caitlin?"

But Caitlin was already asleep.

In a little while, so was everyone else.

He's trying to get me. A monster with a face as white as snow. And fangs. Dracula! He's coming closer and closer. His eyes are red and glowing. He's almost got me. . . .

Alex woke up. She was all sweaty in her sleeping bag. She sat up and pushed her hair off her face.

Something stirred next to her. Becky touched her arm. "What's the matter, Fitzgerald?" she said sleepily. "Can't you sleep?"

"I had a bad dream," Alex whispered. She didn't want the others to hear.

"You ate too much pizza," Becky said. "My dad always says you're not supposed to eat spicy food before you go to bed. Does your stomach hurt? Want a glass of water?"

"No, thanks," said Alex. Her stomach was fine.

"I'll turn on my night-light," mumbled Becky. "That should help you get back to sleep."

"Well, okay," Alex said.

Becky reached over and flipped her night-light on. It had a silly clown face on it.

"Mr. Clown helped me with my bad dreams when I was little," Becky said. Then she rolled over and was asleep.

It took Alex a little longer to fall asleep. Mr. Clown! How babyish could you get? Alex certainly hoped Caitlin and Emily hadn't heard them talking.

Now Alex was more worried than ever. She wondered if this was her *last* slumber party. Who would invite such a baby? What if she was as old as her mom and still had nightmares? It would be *so* embarrassing.

Dear Mom,

How are you? I am fine. I won the tryouts for the Christmas play. I play the piano in it. I have a new best friend, Becky Garcia. She is fine. School is fine. Dad is fine. He is working on a new mushroom diet. I miss you very much.

Love,
Alexandra Fitzgerald

Alex ate another doughnut. Then she wrote:

P.S. Do you know any cures for nightmares?

"Okay, Dad!" Alex called. "I finished my letter. Ready to go to the post office now?"

Alex's dad came out of his office. "Just in time," he said. "I finished a chapter I can mail to my publisher."

Alex and her father left Palm Tree Heaven. They passed by the apartment-complex pool. Alex hadn't gone swimming in it yet. She had a couple of bathing suits. But it seemed too weird to go swimming outside in November.

They walked down the street to the post office.

The post office was bright and sunny. It had flowers all around it. And, of course, many palm trees. Alex sat down under one of them while her father went inside.

Across the street she saw Caitlin and Emily. She waved to them. They came over to say hi.

"My mom is taking us to see *The Slime That Ate San Diego* this afternoon," said Caitlin. "Would you like to come?"

"Alex hates scary movies, remember?" said Emily. She giggled.

Alex felt herself turning red. "Well, thanks. But I have to practice piano," she said. "Yikes, there's my dad—I'll see you guys later!"

She ran off to meet her dad by the doorway. They walked back to Palm Tree Heaven.

"How's that problem we talked about a few weeks ago?" Alex's dad asked. "You know, the bad dreams?"

"I'm still having them," said Alex.

"Alex, are you worried about anything special?" he asked. "Is everything going okay at school? Are you unhappy about anything?"

Alex stared at a woman who was carrying a surfboard and walking a poodle at the same time. The poodle wasn't wearing roller blades, but the woman was.

"Everything is fine," Alex said. "I just need a cure for nightmares."

"Well, I have another idea," said her dad. "You could start writing down your bad dreams."

"Why would I do that?" Alex asked. "It's bad enough just having them."

"If you write them down," he said, "maybe you'll start seeing why you dream about certain things. If you understand them, you'll feel better."

"Sounds good!" said Alex. "Maybe I could write down all my dreams. The good ones, too. That would make it a little more fun."

Back at the apartment, Alex's dad found an old blank notebook she could use. On the notebook's blue cover, Alex wrote

"California Dreamin'." She drew a picture of a palm tree. She didn't write her name on the book. She was the only one who would ever look at it.

Then she put the notebook by her futon. She would start writing in it the very next day.

But that night, she had a bad dream.

Emily and Caitlin and other kids are looking at a blue notebook. It has a palm tree on it. That's my notebook. I want it back! Emily is holding it out of my reach. "What a baby," she says. "Look, a whole book of baby bad dreams!"

"Everyone has bad dreams. . . ." says Elan. His bright red T-shirt reads I LOVE CALIFORNIA GIRLS.

"But only real babies write them down!" says Caitlin. All the kids laugh and laugh.

Alex's mom wrote back right away. She sent a postcard with a colorful painting of Japanese dragons on it. The caption read, "Dragons in China and Japan are thought to be friendly creatures that bring good luck." She wrote:

Dear Alex,
   I miss you very much, too. I am working hard. I can't wait to see you again. It sounds like you are having trouble with nightmares. Go to the

library. There are lots of books about this. You can get some ideas for cures. Also, have you talked to your dad? Have him keep the radio or TV on in the next room while you're falling asleep. Hope this helps. Write back soon!

Love,
Mom

The library! Why hadn't Alex thought of that? What a good idea.

Alex hung her mom's postcard up over her futon. Maybe the dragons would bring *her* good luck.

Alex asked Becky to show her where the school library was the next afternoon. She didn't say why she needed to go. She didn't like to keep secrets from Becky. But she didn't want Becky to know about her big problem. Becky would scream with laughter.

"I have to go to the library, too," said

Becky. "But we have play rehearsal today, remember? How about tomorrow?"

"I have my piano lesson tomorrow," Alex said. "Wednesday?"

Becky shook her head. "I have to work on my geography report. It's due this week. What about Thursday?"

"Colin Ward and I are working on our science project then," said Alex.

"We'll go Friday," said Becky. "For sure."

"For sure," Alex said.

That night, Alex tried her mom's TV idea.

Her dad liked to watch the same show each night. It was a talk show. Usually he kept the volume down low so it wouldn't bother Alex.

Alex asked her dad to turn it up louder while she went to bed.

Alex was almost asleep. Suddenly a voice boomed, "And here's our host for tonight, Larry Lipson!"

Alex tossed and turned.

But she must have fallen asleep, because the next morning she awoke from a dream about Larry Lipson:

"Well, Larry, I'm just thrilled to be here," roars a man with sunglasses and a beard. His orange T-shirt says I'M WHERE THE ACTION IS.

"We're talking to the world-famous artist, Pablo Pablo," Larry Lipson bellows. *"Stay tuned for our next guest, Alex Fitzgerald, who will be talking about her nightmares. . . ."*

Yikes!

Alex stopped her dad in the hallway that morning. "Dad, could you keep the TV down, please?" she said.

"But you asked—" he said.

"Some of us are trying to sleep!" Alex said.

The next two nights Alex tried the radio idea.

It wasn't exactly a cure.

If music came on that she liked, she sang along. That kept her awake. If music came on that she didn't like, she covered her ears. That kept her awake, too.

And on Thursday, while she was working on her science project with Colin Ward, she fell asleep! Colin thought it was funny, but Alex didn't. What if he went around telling everyone?

Meanwhile, she wrote in her notebook each morning. She didn't have any more nightmares to write down.

Till Friday morning. Then she wrote: "Last night Japanese dragons breathed fire all over me. I think they were the dragons from Mom's postcard."

Alex felt terrible. Lunch boxes were bad enough. But how could she turn her very own mom's card into something scary? And what if she started falling asleep during important things—like in the

middle of class, or during a play rehearsal? Alex just had to find a cure now. She grabbed her "California Dreamin'" notebook and ran to meet Becky for school. At least today they were going to the library. Libraries always had the answers!

Alex and Becky were in the school library. Becky went straight to a section marked ANIMAL STORIES.

"I only read books about animals now," she said. "Come and get me when you're ready to go, Fitzgerald."

"Shh," said Mr. Moles, the librarian.

Alex looked around. She carried her "California Dreamin'" notebook with her. She might want to make some notes.

She saw a section marked NIGHTMARES AND OTHER SCARY THINGS. This was it. Alex walked over and set her notebook down. She started looking at the books.

There was a book called *Vampire Bats Are Coming to Get You.* Another book called *Don't Look Under Your Bed—or Else!* Alex shuddered. One called *Night of the Living Bed,* and one called *Monsters from Beyond the Grave.* Yikes!

These were books to *give* a person nightmares. Alex couldn't imagine wanting to read such books. She was trying to get *rid* of nightmares.

Alex walked up to the librarian's desk. "Do you have any books to help a kid stop having bad dreams?" She spoke softly. She didn't want anyone else to hear her.

"Excuse me?" said Mr. Moles.

Alex repeated her question. A little louder this time.

"Sure," Mr. Moles said. He led Alex to the far corner of the library.

She watched while he picked out a few

books from the shelves. A little boy looked up at her. Alex recognized him. He was a first grader.

Alex felt herself turning beet red. She was in the little-kid section!

"Take a look at these," Mr. Moles said. "These should help your little brother or sister. Let me know if you need more help." He walked back to his desk.

Alex started looking at the books. They were mostly all pictures. One was about a boy who thought there were monsters under his bed. Another was about a girl who was scared of the dark. All the kids in the books were very little.

"I used to have nightmares all the time, too," someone said.

Alex jumped. It was the first-grade boy.

"But my grandma helped me stop," the boy said.

"Oh? How?" Alex asked.

"She told me to think happy thoughts,"

said the boy. "You could tell your little brother or sister to remember something good while falling asleep."

"Well, thanks," said Alex.

She left the books on the table and went to get Becky. She felt disappointed. The library was no help, after all. She was going to have to find a cure somewhere else.

The two girls left the library. They walked to the school's front door.

"Alexandra Fitzgerald and Rebecca Garcia!" It was Ms. Chung, director of the Christmas play. She sounded mad. "Where were you two?" she asked. "I called an extra rehearsal this afternoon."

"Yikes!" Alex said. "I forgot all about it."

"Me, too," Becky said.

"You and half the cast forgot about it," Ms. Chung said.

"We're sorry—" said Becky.

"We've just been so busy—" Alex said.

"Don't let this happen again. I'll see you

at rehearsal on Monday." Ms. Chung walked off down the hall.

Later that night, Alex realized that she'd forgotten something else besides the rehearsal. She was getting ready for bed. She went to put her "California Dreamin'" notebook next to her futon, as usual.

But it was missing.

She had lost her private, personal, very important notebook.

First thing Monday morning, Alex went back to the library. She couldn't find her notebook anywhere. Mr. Moles hadn't seen it, either.

So that night, she decided she might as well try out the idea from the little boy in the library. His grandma said to think quiet, happy thoughts before going to bed.

At first it seemed to work. Alex thought about last Christmas, all snowy and white in Chicago. She had gone ice-skating with her friends. It was the most fun she ever had. . . .

But one night, she dreamed about a vampire bat coming to get her. And another night, she dreamed monsters were crawling around under her bed. In another dream, a grandmother popped out from behind a tombstone and screeched, "Don't worry, be happy!"

The morning after that dream, Alex woke up and burst out laughing. She wasn't scared. These were dreams about what she had found in the library. Her mom's idea had sure backfired. Instead of curing her nightmares, the library was *giving* her nightmares! It was funny. Well, almost funny.

Alex celebrated Thanksgiving with her dad. She helped him make a turkey with mushroom stuffing.

She stayed overnight at Becky's house every Saturday night now. Sometimes Caitlin or Emily invited her over, too. Once they asked her to go to a movie—not a scary one. This time Alex went.

Another day, all four girls went to the beach. It felt weird to go to the beach in December. Alex wouldn't go swimming. But she loved watching the surfers.

"Someday," she told the other girls, "I'm going to learn to surf, too."

"We'll believe *that* when we see you swim," Becky said.

Rehearsals for the play were twice a week now. Sometimes they got noisy. But not when Alex sat down to play her piano solo. Then everyone in the cast was quiet. Even the stage crew stayed quiet while Alex played.

One day Alex outdid herself. Everyone applauded when she was through. She turned beet red. But inside she was thrilled. She had been practicing hard, and it really showed.

"You are the greatest!" said Caitlin

after rehearsal. "The best part of the play."

"I could take piano lessons for a million years," said Emily, "and I'd never play as well as you."

"Well, thanks," said Alex.

"Don't get conceited, Fitzgerald," said Becky. "You have to tell us how good we are, too." She punched Alex's arm lightly.

"The dancers *are* really good," said Alex. "But watch out for my arm. That's my piano arm."

Then Becky, Emily, and Caitlin took turns poking Alex's arm. All four girls were giggling.

Soon it was the middle of December. At rehearsal one day, Alex sat down to play her piano solo as usual. She opened up her music as usual.

Then she gulped.

On the first page of her music, someone had written "babyfingers" in red crayon.

Quickly Alex flipped through the rest of her music. "Babyfingers" was scrawled all over every page!

Alex didn't know what to do. She played her piece as usual. She tried not to cry.

But inside, her mind was in a whirl. Someone had wrecked her music. Who? And why?

Alex could think of only one answer: The kids in her school had found her secret "California Dreamin'" notebook. Now they were teasing her about her babyish bad dreams.

Alex's *worst* nightmare was coming true.

After rehearsal, Alex walked home with Becky.

"Someone played a mean joke on me," Alex said. She showed Becky her music.

"That's horrible!" said Becky. "Who would do that?"

"Someone who thinks I'm a baby," Alex said. "Do you think it might be Caitlin or Emily?"

"What? You're crazy, Fitzgerald. Caitlin and Emily really like you. All they talk about is how great you are."

"I know," said Alex. She was silent for a minute. "But remember your slumber party at Halloween? When I had that nightmare?"

"And I turned on my night-light?" asked Becky.

"Right. I think Caitlin and Emily heard us talking that night."

"I don't think so," Becky said. "And even if they did, so what?"

"Well, I've had a few other nightmares besides that one," said Alex. She could feel her heart pounding.

"I'm sorry to hear it," Becky said. "But who else would know that besides you?"

Alex sighed. Then she told Becky about her whole secret problem. About all the different cures she had tried. About the "California Dreamin'" notebook, and how she had lost it that day at the library.

"Maybe someone did find your notebook," said Becky. "Maybe someone is teasing you. But it's not Caitlin or Emily. I'm positive."

"I hope not," said Alex. They were at the gate to Palm Tree Heaven.

"But, hey! I have a great idea for a cure," Becky said. "This Saturday night, I'll let you sleep with my worry dolls."

"No, thanks," said Alex. "I've got my own Barbie dolls."

"No, Fitzgerald, *worry* dolls. My parents brought me a set of worry dolls from their last trip to Mexico. They're teeny tiny. You tell them your worries before you go to sleep. Then you stick them under your pillow. While you sleep, the dolls solve your problems."

"You're kidding," Alex said.

"Well, it's worth a try. I've been using the dolls all week. Remember my lunch box? The one with the picture from *Aliens You Love to Hate?*"

"Yes, I remember it," Alex said. She

didn't tell Becky she'd had dreams about it. Becky didn't have to know everything. "Though I haven't seen it lately. Did you give it to your little brother?"

"I *lost* it," Becky said. "And my mom is going to *kill* me if I don't find it. I hoped the worry dolls would help me think of where I put it. But I'll let you use them Saturday night. No problem."

"Well, thanks," Alex said.

"They should work for nightmares," Becky went on. "The dolls will get them instead of you. You'll be cured!"

Alex was ready to try anything. She was getting desperate.

On Saturday night, Alex slept over at Becky's house.

The worry dolls were cute and colorful. HANDMADE IN GUATEMALA read the sticker on their box. There were six of them. Each one wasn't much bigger than a fingernail.

Alex tried not to feel silly as she talked to the dolls about her nightmares. Then she put them under her pillow.

Alex didn't have any nightmares that night. That was because she didn't have much sleep that night.

The dolls were so very small. What if she fell asleep and one of them went up her nose? Or in her eye or ear? What if she rolled over on the dolls and crushed them?

Alex lay awake most of the night. Worrying . . . about the worry dolls.

"Up your nose?" Becky hooted. "In your ear?"

It was the next morning. Alex and Becky couldn't stop giggling.

"Fitzgerald, you're amazing," Becky said. "You can turn *any* cure into a disaster!"

"I know," Alex said. She tried to feel sorry for herself. But actually, she didn't feel too bad. It was good to share her secret problem with a friend. Even if the friend's idea for a cure was a disaster.

And she had gotten up that morning with a couple of good ideas of her own. She knew what she had to do.

There was a play rehearsal on Monday after school. Before it began, Alex went over to Ms. Chung. Alex opened her music to show the "babyfingers" written on every page.

"Someone did this to my music last week," Alex said shakily.

"This is a disgrace!" Ms. Chung clapped her hands loudly. "I want the attention of the entire cast and stage crew, please! I'd like to know who is responsible for vandalizing Alexandra Fitzgerald's music."

There was only silence. Boys and girls looked shocked.

"Right now!" said Ms. Chung.

A red-faced boy stepped forward. He wore a black T-shirt that said LET'S PARTY, DUDE!

"Elan Kent!" said Ms. Chung. "Do you know who did this?"

"Someone who wanted to play piano for the Christmas play," Elan mumbled. "He told me he did it. He thought . . . He thought if he scared Alex, she would quit the play. Then he'd get a chance."

Alex didn't know what to say. She was pretty sure Elan was the "someone." But that meant that the "babyfingers" had nothing to do with her nightmares or her secret notebook.

What a relief!

"Elan, I'll speak to you in my office after rehearsal," said Ms. Chung. "Alexandra— everyone—take your places. Start the rehearsal!"

After the rehearsal was over, Alex took action on her second idea.

She dragged Becky down the hall to the school's Lost and Found room. "Let's find your lost lunch box," she said. "I don't want your mom to kill you."

Sure enough, the *Aliens* lunch box was there.

"Fitzgerald, you're better than a worry doll!" said Becky. She poked Alex in the arm.

Something else was there, too. A blue notebook. With a palm tree on the front. And "California Dreamin'" written on it.

"Yikes!" said Alex.

"It must have been here since the day you lost it at the library," Becky said.

"And I didn't write my name on it," Alex said. "So no one knew it was mine. No one could return it to me."

"And no one knows about your bad dreams!" Becky pointed out.

The two girls grabbed their things. They ran out of the school building and into the sunny California afternoon.

"I was thinking about your nightmare

problem," said Becky on the way home. "You know, I just remembered a great cure—"

Alex wasn't really paying attention. She was thinking that she hadn't *had* a real nightmare in a while. A couple of weeks now.

It was hard to believe, but maybe she had cured *herself.* Just by growing a little bit older.

"Tell me another time," Alex said to Becky. "Right now, let's go for a swim! You can borrow my extra bathing suit."

"No problem!" said Becky.

The two girls raced each other to Palm Tree Heaven.